UNFORESEEN PARTITIONS

BY KEETA B.

Steamy Trails Publishing:
www.steamytrailspublishing.com

ISBN-13:978-0-692-53309-3

ISBN-10: 0692533095

Dedication

To all the people in the world that want a little more spice back in their lives or perhaps even a little love and lust to bring out your inner freak…loosen up, take a seat and allow *Unforeseen Partition* sizzle to revitalize your senses and put thoughts into actions.

Acknowledgements

Very special thanks to my sister, Keybae, for participating in my second book and to my subscribers for following and encouraging my literary journey. And last but not least, thanks to my publisher, Steamy Trails Publishing, for another great read!

Contents

Introduction

Unforeseen Partitions is a collaboration of erotic short stories and poetry that is intended to heighten your sexual senses, question your quest for love and leave you wanting more. The opening poem introduces my beloved sister, Keybae. She is a new writer and I am extremely proud to be collaborating with her.

She perfectly sets the mode to explicit compilation of poetry and short stories. We hope you enjoy what this book holds as this is only the beginning of our working together.

I Want That

by Keybae

Baby I've already told you I want what you want

But let me tell you again I want your dick

He tells me it's nothing in this world that sounds more beautiful than hearing me say that I want his dick

Now I can't let my girls influence me by telling me such a request is wrong

Cause you know and I know you can't give me that dick without giving me that tongue

So why would you settle for less? Unless you're cool with not getting the best

And if that is the case I suggest you don't seek me to ya mess

Cause messing with me could mean trouble

And this pussy will mess around and have you seeing doubles

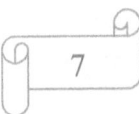

So let me make your day, better yet make your night

Better yet I'll make your week, only if that is alright

So you know what we need to do

Baby did I tell you how much I want your dick?

Oh damn, he just love hearing me say how much I want his dick

And if I want his dick, his dick is exactly what I'm going to get

That frozen chocolate pipe look alike is exactly what I'm gone get

Now I just want you to know I want your dick

I don't know what's wrong with me but it's just something about your dick

I mean what could be better than me enjoying your dick?

If you asked anybody that I done in my past,
they'll tell you it's something about what I
do with that dick

I got one third of your dick in my hand and
the other two thirds in my mouth

Fuck that, you know how gifted I am let me
take my hand out of the equation and put ya
whole dick in my mouth

Just trying to make you smile baby even if I
don't succeed

Just you watching me trying to swallow
your whole dick is making it harder for you
to breath

But who gives a fuck, right now that really
don't matter

So try to get yourself together

I got to be honest with you baby I love
sucking your dick

It got me to the point where I can't wait until
your sucking on my clit

And your fingers working my hole

And my hands on top of your head

And your voice telling me to take control

No need for me to be stunnin, you got my
eyeliner runnin

No need for lying baby, your head got me
crying baby

You got me screaming for that long stroke

But not before I'm cumming all down your
throat

Yasss, that's what you fucking get

Did I tell you how much it turns me on to
hear you say you love licking on this clit

Did I tell you how you have the best head in
the south?

You got this warm, creamy, delicious
substance melting right in your mouth

Damn you got my clit feeling sick

Fuck a love letter

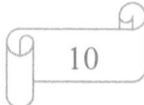

How about you just keep on sucking cause
two shots of me should make it feel better

Now let me be your dick doctor for a
moment, but I need you to do what the
doctor ordered

Let me get you to full attention

Look on the side of your dick its written
multiple refills on that prescription

Keybae!!

Betrayal

While sitting in my office, I received a phone call and it's Jason.

Jason, my ex-partner, who I kept in contact with since my departure from the force; Jason O'Connell was a good friend and confidant. He vowed to keep the case open and find out who shot me and why they have not been apprehended.

Jason, in his deep baritone voice asked, "How's it going Faith? I'm hoping you're in good spirits."

"Thank you for asking, I'm actually doing well," I replied.

"I mean how are you really doing, Faith? You always seem to be here at the office or teaching one of those Self Defense classes," said Jason.

"I said I'm doing well, Jason. What do you want to hear?"

I was beginning to get agitated with this line of questioning, but it was not Jason's fault.

"I have some new information regarding your case. We have had a new private eye on surveillance and he gave me a package to give to you," Jason said.

"Sounds good, let's meet over lunch. We have some catching up to do anyways," I replied.

We decided to meet at a quiet little bistro located downtown on Lamar Ave and 126th Street. The sun was covered by the clouds and it was a tad bit hazy with a slight mist in the air. The fall breeze was blowing softly. I arrived around 1:30 p.m. and chose a table by the window looking out into Community Park. The flowers with all beautiful arrays of color were still in bloom. I found myself daydreaming, staring at my reflection through the glass window, when Jason arrived and walked over to the table; he slightly touched my shoulder for me to acknowledge his presence.

I hadn't spoken with Jason in over three months due to him being undercover and involved in a stake out. It put a smile on my face to see him and I was excited to know he wasn't hurt or in any danger. The life of a cop can be hard sometimes when you're trying to catch the bad guy.

We sat, and ate our lunch then caught up on how my Self Defense classes were going.

Since retiring from the police force I took on a full-time position as a Self Defense Instructor. My first class began at 6:30 a.m. This class was an advance one. I had a class of ten active duty policemen, three school teachers and a few elderly that attended the early session. In my second class of the day, I taught anyone who worked in a law enforcement type capacity (i.e. police department, security, private or commercial). I did this 3-4 times a week, depending on the need of the community.

It had been almost two years since I was critically wounded on the job which ended my career.

I was on a stake out with my fellow officers trying to bust a gambling ring when I was shot three times. I was hit by one of the bullets; it went straight through my left shoulder, another one went through my right lower abdominal area, while the third bullet nicked my spine causing my legs to give way from under me, leaving me hospitalized for over three months while trying to learn to walk again and digest the fact I would never be able to work as an undercover agent again. I was damaged goods.

To lighten the mood Jason changed the conversation. He knew I got upset talking about what happened to me. Especially, since I was permanently left with a limp. He knew that being a lame bothered me.

"Have you found anyone special to spend your down time with?" Jason asked in an awkward manner. His shoulders were stiff, face was turned up and eyes crossed. He was almost blushing.

I asked myself, "How did I know this question was coming and from my best friend?"

"No, Jason I have not found anyone. I'm still single and will remain that way for a very long time."

Looking stunned Jason twisted his mouth for another question. I quickly interrupted his train of thought.

"Don't look at me like that, Jason; you how I feel about dating, trust, and the whole ordeal of getting to know someone intimately. Being shot really did a number on me and I enjoy my life exactly the way it is...ALONE."

Jason looked at me once again this time with a smirk on his face. He knew he was pushing my buttons.

"You may not be looking or even expect it but the right man for you is going to appear and sweep you off your feet whether you like it or not."

"Enough of that funny business, tell me about the information you may have for me regarding my case." I said.

"No problem, but let's first take a walk through the park for a few minutes," said Jason.

As we were about to get up from the table I heard a familiar voice but couldn't tell where it was coming from. I looked all around when as we were approaching the exit we bumped right into him. It was my brother Robert. Normally, he would rush and give me that sisterly bear hug, but today he seemed a bit nervous and out of place. He gave me small talk and was a bit startled, so I asked him what brought him to this side of town when he worked 25 minutes from here.

"You know good food will make a man drive several miles when he's hungry sis," replied Robert in a melodramatic way.

He then gave me a quick hug and rushed out the door.

"Wow that was strange. I've never seen Robert act in such a manner."

"Oh Faith, you read too much into stuff, maybe he was just extremely hungry," chuckled Jason.

"I sure hope so." I replied.

We continued walking out of the bistro and to the park across the street.

"I didn't want to share any information I may have in a place where anyone could over hear us talking," said Jason.

"Must be some heavy stuff you and that private eye have been uncovering," I concurred.

We found a park bench and had a seat. We briefly went over the night I was shot and the turn of events that went on leading up to that night. Jason informed me about the group of racketeering ring leaders that were under surveillance and a few more suspects involved with the gambling ring. He then handed me a manila envelope and told me not to open it until I was in a safe place and could examine all the contents thoroughly.

After my last class of the day I arrived back home and took a quick shower and grabbed a bite to eat. I turned on my 70 inch flat screen television to create some noise in the house, and then I plopped down on the Mocha color Italian leather couch to make myself comfortable. I opened the manila folder and took all of its contents out and placed them on the coffee table in front of me. The very first page contained an FBI information sheet with my personal information on it. While reading the information I come across something that caught my eye and caused me to look closer. While examining the form I notice the name of the assailant, and his place of employment. My brother being the only Robert I knew who worked for the company so my initial thoughts was:

"It couldn't be the Robert I know. Not my Robert."

FBI INFORMATION DATA SHEET

COMMENTS: AGENT BUCCHAN WAS SHOT WHILE ON STAKEOUT. SUSPECTS: ROLLINS GANG/

PRO-TECH CORPORATION. DUE TO HER INJURIES SHE WAS FORCED TO RESIGN FROM THE PD. ON ASSIGNMENT

18 MONTHS. POI: ROBERT B. AKA THE HITMAN (ASSAILANT NOT CAPTURED)

Also, inside the envelope were several incriminating pictures. I examined each one and was surprised by what I saw. While sitting on the couch, I was speaking to myself and I was mesmerized. I couldn't believe who I saw in the majority of the photographs.

"Why was my brother Robert in any of these pictures"?

I flipped through several more items that were in the pile and noticed an update on the case and it was labeled,

"TOP CONFIDENTIAL". I read the notes over and over to make sure I was reading it correctly. Someone had put out a hit on me. They truly wanted me dead.

I pushed the papers off the coffee table, balled up on the couch and began to sob, rocking back and forth. This can't be what I think. My own brother was the assailant I've been looking for all this time.

"How could he do this? What has he gotten himself into?" I wondered.

Just the thought of my own brother trying to kill me had my stomach in knots. The reoccurring dreams I was having of the man in the mask, and him standing over me looking as though his conscious was bothering him. The guilt of not knowing who it was leaves the question of why? Why would my own flesh and blood place a hit out on my life? I just can't believe this.

I got up off the couch, and searched for my cell phone. I needed someone to talk to before I lost my mind.

I had to call the one person I knew would understand, Jason. He answered on the first ring. He could hear the frustration in my voice and agreed to come over and talk. What seemed like forever, Jason finally arrived and knocked on the door. Once I let him in we walked into the kitchen and had a seat.

"I got here as quick as I could. Is everything alright?" Jason asked.

"No, everything is not okay. Someone tried to put a hit out on my life, and tell me why my brother is in the majority of those pictures you gave me." I yelled. "I need some answers." My arms were flailing around in the air.

Jason bowed his head and cupped his hands together. He leaned back on the bar stool and slowly began speaking.

"Faith, you were my partner for over 6 years. I never expected in a million years for you to get hurt. All I wanted to do was to protect you and I failed at that one.

Your brother is in the majority of those pictures because he's the one who was hired to kill you."

"No, Jason. That's not true. Stop lying to me and give me the truth," I demanded.

"It's all true Faith. Robert was hired to kill you. Do you remember the night at the warehouse after you had been shot? You said someone stood over you with a mask and stared. Surveillance captured that moment and also the moment when he walked away and removed his mask. This is how we found out who the 'Hit man' really was."

Furiously I stated, "Why in the hell didn't anyone ever tell me they suspected my brother as the hit man? He was at the hospital after I was shot, sometimes 3-4 times a day. Was this so he could report back to whomever the status of my condition?" "Why would he do this to his own sister?"

Jason stood up from the bar stool and walked over to where I was.

He wrapped his arms around me to console me. I couldn't do anything I was numb so I wrapped my arms around his waist and shared the embrace with him.

He then in a soft spoken voice replied, "He has a gambling problem and is part of the Pro-Tech cartel. Robert has been under investigation for the last 2 years. We first thought it was his wife who was involved but after watching her for over 6 months we found out her hands were clean. Her activities were basic ones and she never owned a gun. Ballistics came back and she was cleared of all suspicions. However, your brother owns several guns and they have been fired recently. It was a shame; your sister-in-law doesn't really know her own husband and what his outside activities are."

Faith, still in shock, looked up at Jason with tear filled eyes and said, "Why didn't you as my partner tell me about my brother? You're my best friend, so why would you keep this from me?"

I stared into Jason's deep brown eyes seeking the answers I needed. He has never kept anything from me before.

Jason was speechless and had trouble finding the right choice of words. He had to clear his throat to dislodge the lump that had formed, and then began to speak.

"I didn't tell you because I love you Faith and didn't want you to suffer any more than you already have. I knew if you found out it would devastate you, and I couldn't sit and watch that happen to the woman I love so passionately."

Looking around in a daze, I couldn't believe my ears. I was at a loss for words. I didn't know how to respond to what my best friend, my confidant had just said to me. Deep down inside I know I have some feelings, I just don't know what they are at this point.

I was confused. Did Jason just confess his love for me and that he protected me from finding out who tried to kill me for my own well-being? I don't know how to take all this information in. What's really going on here?

"Why after all this time of being friends, he just now decided to confess his feelings?"

"All I know is I need to find my brother and have a few words with him. I need to get to the bottom of this once and for all."

"I don't think that would be a good idea, Faith." Jason responded. "That day at the bistro we had undercover agents in the place and they discovered Jason was making another big money deal. When you said he seemed startled when we were leaving the bistro. You were right. He owes a lot of money to several people and they are ready to collect. Robert was instructed to kill you or be killed."

"You're in a lot of danger and I won't sit back and allow you to be hurt again. There is another meeting at the old warehouse in a couple days. The cartel and Robert will make a transaction. I can have you tag along for when we make the bust and you can confront him then."

I paced the floor over and over. Overwhelmed and shocked from the news of finding out my brother was responsible for ending my career, and my longtime partner had fallen in love with me. I'm not ready for any of this. However, on the other hand I need to find out why Robert would be involved in the cartels gambling activities putting not only me in danger but our entire family.

The night of the cartel meeting I prepared myself for the worst. I prayed to God to give me strength to accept whatever happened on tonight. Jason picked me up around 8 p.m. in an unmarked squad car. I was dressed in a black Nike wind suit with all black sneakers and a baseball cap. I had my hair pulled up and tucked securely under the hat so no one could notice me. When we arrived to the warehouse we drove to the back of it and parked the car. My heart began to race as if I was having a panic attack. Visions of the night I was fatally shot flashed before my eyes. Jason could tell I was a bit nervous so he grabbed my hand and held on tight then looked me in the eyes to see if I was alright. I assured him I would be.

"Let's just get this over with so we can go home." I said.

We got out the car and entered the building through a side door. We climbed the stairs and my leg began to ache and began to tingle from the nerve damage. We found an upper level deck overlooking the warehouse where the cartel had set up a meeting table and some chairs. We sat quietly for several minutes observing. I spotted Robert when he first walked in followed by 3 more men all dressed in business suits. Once everyone was seated at the table they began a discussion about how much money was going to be exchanged for services. A tall bald-headed olive colored man stood from the table and pointed his gun at my brother. He started yelling something we couldn't understand.

All I could make out of it was, "Why didn't you kill the cop off like you were instructed to do the first time. You cost us a lot of money by not killing that nosey bitch."

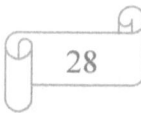

Robert didn't have time to respond before shots rang out in the place. I then heard someone yell out, "Shots fired, invade the premises."

The FBI and undercover local police rushed in and also began firing. After all the shooting and smoke cleared I rushed down the stairs to check on Robert. He was lying on the floor in a pool of blood barely breathing. As I looked around everyone else was dead or in just as bad of a condition. I kicked the gun away from Robert before I approached him. I kneeled down beside him and pulled him close to me. He had been shot in the left shoulder and right thigh. Tears had filled my eyes once again.

"Why, Robert? How could you be involved in something like this? How could you try to kill your own sister?"

There was silence; Robert turned his head away from me as if to be ignoring me.

"Dammit! Say something; tell me why you would ruin my career over money and greed."

Robert grasping onto his breath could only muster up enough energy to say, "Because I'm not you sis. I'm not a goody two shoes with my nose all up in air. I needed the money for all the gambling debt I had incurred since college and it caught up with me."

"I'm sorry Faith. I really am sorry."

I looked my brother square in the eyes and replied, "Sorry isn't enough this time Robert, I'll see you on visitation day, behind bars."

Tears rolled down my face as I turned and walked away from Robert. All the anger I once felt was no longer. I felt free.

Motioning for Jason, "Let's go home we have some unfinished business there, it's time we start a new chapter."

Jason put his arm around me and smiled. He then planted the sloppiest kiss on me ever. I was excited to have closed one chapter of my life so I can start anew. He was excited I was ready to try something I had been avoiding for a long time; us being together.

Hidden Walls

What's hidden behind a cloth?

And not made seen

Leaves the eyes to wonder

On what could be.

Hidden behind these walls

An image unclear

Walls that stands so tall

Leaving only the imagination

To see.

Hidden walls so tall

We can barely see,

What's inside your heart?

That built these walls so tall,

Is it dreams…

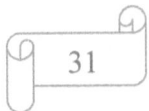

That roams freely?

I say to you,

Uncover your eyes

And there you'll find

Where the answer to your questions

And true love lies.

Cyber Love

Here I am sitting at this damn computer again. It's a Friday night and I have nothing to do.

"I really need a social life," Marissa said to herself.

Why is it, I'm on almost every single dating site known to man, and every social media and still single? No one ever asks me out on dates or shows any interest in me? I'm attractive: being olive complexion, long black hair, big brown doe eyes, high cheek bones and full lips. I'm smart having graduated top of my high school and college class. Now I have a full time career as a Supervisor over the Bio-engineering department at the local hospital. I'm a very caring person and I love giving back to the community, but for some reason men see me as a threat. I've tried everything but I'm far from desperate. A co-work told me about cyber dating and even gave me a few of the sites to try.   I guess it wouldn't hurt I could give it a try.

Monday mornings are hectic for me.   It seems like all I do is go from one meeting to another all day long. When I finally got a moment to check my computer I noticed I had over twenty messages in my inbox. They were from names and e-mail addresses I had never seen before.   I was in shock almost to the point I thought it was spam mail.   I began opening up each entry and noticed they were from the cyber dating site I had opened up my profile on the night before.   I couldn't believe it. All these men had noticed my profile in that short amount of time and wanted to correspond with me. I was ecstatic.

I began by answering each message as if I was some type of school girl who has never been on a date.   It must have been all the attention that had me flattered. Honestly, I haven't been on a date in over two years or in a serious relationship in over ten. Here it is I'm a 34 year old educated woman with a lot to offer but I can't seem to attract or keep a man. I was beginning to just give up and

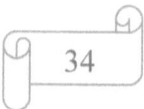

say "fuck it" on the whole idea of dating or men altogether but I promised Sarah my co-worker I wouldn't throw in the towel just yet. Sarah told me I was too young to have that mind set on not dating and giving up. I'm vibrant and I need to live and enjoy life. She also reminded me that someone would come along I would have to be patient.

My very first e-mail response was from this guy name Tyrone. Tyrone described himself as 38, tall 6'0, dark complexion, slender, muscular built, bald, athletic and very charming. He also says he's an independent pharmacist. I asked what he was looking for in a lady friend he responded:

"I'm looking for an attractive woman who knows how to have an educated conversation, one who knows when, and how to lead without being told and an independent woman who isn't afraid of help when it's given to her." replied Tyrone.

I liked what I was reading about this man already, but I better not get my hopes up too soon he could be a wolf in sheep's clothing.

Moving on to the next e-mail; it was from a guy named Max. Max was this half Black, half Puerto Rican guy. Max informed me that he was a 36 year old Communication's Manager at a Radio Station. He then described himself as medium build, 5'10, fair complexion, dark wavy hair, and devoted. He loves to listen to music, dance and teaches kick-boxing part-time and was recently divorced. I also asked Max the same question I did Tyrone what he was looking for in a lady friend. He responded,

"One who can entice my mind, body and soul? I want a woman who encourages her man and motivates him to succeed in whatever he chooses to do. I'm also looking for a lady who will be my soul-mate, my companion, my equal, and my best friend."

Wow, Max was getting real deep on me; I almost lost self-control from just reading his message. Hmm, I'd better log off this computer and do some work before I get myself in trouble.

Time had slipped by me. What felt like a few minutes ended being several hours and then it hit me, I hadn't taken my lunch break yet and boy was I starving. I decided I would go to Jason's Deli and have a soup and salad for lunch. I was surprised for a Monday it wasn't as busy as I thought it would be. I decided I would dine in and relax for a while before heading back to the hospital. Choosing a quiet corner far in the back, I pulled out my iPad and cell phone and checked my messages while I ate my lunch. I read several of the other messages I had received and checked out the profiles held by those individuals. There were two more guys with whom I decided I would reply back. I know I would need to narrow down my choice to at least two soon but their responses would be the determining factor.

The first of my two choices I responded to was TJ. TJ was 35, bright complexion, short wavy hair, 6'2 and a personal chef. TJ said his favorite dish to fix was anything Caribbean or of a Jamaican origin. He stated, "He loves to show his lady a good time and take her out to see the town and do things that couples do. He also informed me that he had no problem staying at home in a pair of sweat pants and t-shirt watching a movie and eating popcorn if that's how the night presents itself." TJ also told me he's an only child and how he loves kids and often volunteers at the foster homes.

Justin was the final candidate I would choose from. He worked as a civil engineer for the Daimler Chrysler Corporation. He was in charge of operations and making sure the plant ran smoothly. Justin stated he was six foot even, 200 pounds of solid muscle and loved dancing and rock music. Justin's parents were creole and originally from Louisiana. Cooking was his second passion and the scent of a woman is what attracts him. His skin complexion is medium brown and he has freckles across his nose, his eyes are sunk in his head and deep brown in color. He wears his hair short on the sides and a Mohawk in the middle. Justin says that when he's alone with a woman it's all about her and what she wants, he believes in pleasing his women in any way possible. He loves the chase and especially loves the reaction the women give him from his pampering. This fellow could be a keeper all by himself.

It was getting harder and harder deciding which man to choose from to go out on a date with. All of them had qualities that peak my interest, and I don't have time to go out with all of them. Hmm, maybe I can ask each one to meet me for a drink after work or something. That way I can meet each candidate in person and make my choice on which one I would like to see on a regular basis. Sitting at my desk contemplating on my next move I decided to e-mail each guy and do as I had suggested, "Yeah, I can do that, it won't hurt anyone and we can all meet face to face."

It wasn't long before I started receiving responses to my e-mails. Each one had agreed to meet at the specific times and date. Maybe they thought as if I did that it wouldn't hurt having a small drink after work. We decided on a local bar located inside of a prestigious hotel on 159th Street and Coolidge. It was in the heart of downtown and not that far from the hospital. My co-workers and I used to go there all the time after work. It had good food, music, and the drinks were strong as hell. Everyone seemed to enjoy the cozy atmosphere. Then I stopped showing up and the rest of the bunch did too. My co-workers claim I was to blame for the group falling apart, but I beg to differ. My work load just increased and I wasn't able to hang out with them as much as I used to, but that wasn't any reason for them to stop going. I wasn't sure how I should feel about this; nor if I should have feeling at all. We all have a good time when we hung out together, but I am the supervisor and my work comes first.

Late one Wednesday afternoon I met with Tyrone. Due to the both of our schedules not permitting a long dinner we decided to just have a glass of wine and a sandwich. Our meeting lasted approximately 20 minutes and we had a chance to see one another face to face and exchange more information about ourselves. We found out we were both workaholics and enjoyed our careers to the fullest. Tyrone seemed mesmerized by my natural beauty and made mention of it several times. Tyrone complimented me on how wonderful I looked and how beautiful my eyes were. He told me my skin complexion accentuated my big doe eyes. Tyrone also told me how he enjoys my personality and could tell we would get along great together. Feeling flattered and embarrassed at the same time by his words I politely said, "Thank you." My cheeks were beet red from him staring. I had never received so many compliments in one day by a man before. I suggested we finish our drinks and part ways. Tyrone asked me to call him later; I agreed to do just that.

Not trying to seem overly impressed I waited a few days before I called Tyrone back. Our conversation continued where it left off and I was ecstatic about the things he was telling me. I truly felt like a school girl who just went on her first date. I don't know what I'm going to do but he sure was making it hard for me to make a decision. There were still three other guys who I needed to go out with before making my final decision. This dating thing is harder than I anticipated.

The following week I decided to have an early brunch with Max. We choose to meet at a local Mom and Pops restaurant since we both had board meeting this particular day and the rest of the week was hectic for the both of us. We sat down at a table located near the rear corner window. We greeted with a firm hug and small peck on the cheek. Max pulled out my chair for me then sat cross from me with his leg crossed. We talked about Max's part-time job teaching kick boxing. He informed me this has always been a passion for him as well as a stress reliever. Max told me as a kid he had some anger issues and his parents thought this was a great way for him to release some of that anger. He admitted it actually worked by time he was a teenager he had learned how to be in control of his anger. Amazed by his confession about his past I also admitted my shyness growing up. Telling this person about my life was something I wasn't used to doing. Almost feeling ashamed about being shy as a kid I thought it would be a turn off to him. Max just laughed and smiled then said, "Don't feel ashamed about being shy, its normal for kids to be that way growing up." That statement made me feel a little better about myself. We finished up our conversation and headed to our meetings that were in the next twenty minutes or so. Max walked me to my car where he planted a kiss on my cheek then headed off down the block.

"Narrowing down who I was going to date was getting harder and harder by the minute. I've been on two dates so far and they both seem to be wonderful men."

As I did with Tyrone I waited a few days before calling Max back after our date. He had attempted to call me several times but I was tied up each time. It was to a point we were playing phone tag with one another. When he finally received my call he seems overjoyed with excitement. Max inquired if I saw it at all possible for us to go on a more romantic date in the near future. I wasn't sure of the correct answer but I was most definite we would see each other again. My response to Max, "I'm sure we could make that happen sometime or another." "Great that would be perfect, just let me know when you're available again and I'll set something up." Max replied.

Still having two more dates I needed to go on I wasn't quite sure when I would be getting back to Max but he surely was a contender for the final round.

Several weeks went by before I had an opportunity to get with my other two options. Work had gotten a little hectic. The hospital had cut our funding so several people were laid off. That meant the remaining people had to carry the load of those laid off. It caused for longer working hours and seven day work weeks. However, I didn't totally blow any of these men off we communicated via text message and e-mails. They all said they understood work came first and play second and for me not to worry they would wait for me until I'm available. They never seemed to let me down. Each one of them in their own way was making an everlasting impression on me.

While at work late one Friday evening I had gotten a text message from one of the prospects I hadn't had the opportunity to go out with yet TJ. TJ expressed his concerned on the amount of time it's been since I had agreed to have a date with him. He inquired if I was too busy to go have that drink at the local bar inside of the hotel. Only having a few more reports to run and could finish them at home I agreed to meet him there in half an hour. Putting the finishing touches on the report I was currently working on I put the remainder two in my briefcase, stepped from behind my desk and went into the restroom located inside my office to change clothes and freshen up. It had truly been a long day and this drink would be good to help me wind down. TJ had already arrived by time I made it to the hotel. Parking seemed a tad bit heavy tonight for some reason. TJ was wearing a black single button blazer, with a sky blue dress shirt, khaki slacks and rustic color Stacy Adams loafers. Once he noticed me he rose from the bar stool he was sitting on and approached me with open arms for an embrace. I obliged and return the gesture. I almost lost myself from his embrace. It was tantalizing. The way he snuggled his face into my neck was so sensual and invigorating. After we released each other from the embrace he grabbed my hand and spun me around to admire my attire. Wearing a red, low cut A-line dress, with silver Jimmy Choo pumps and matching clutch purse. This man was demonstrating every woman's description of compassionate. He then walked me back to where he was sitting at the bar. He had already ordered a Hennessey and Coke for him and me an Apple Martini. We talked and laughed and reminisced about childhood memories. TJ spoke about his job and his upcoming events. My story wasn't nearly as exciting as his but he still seemed to enjoy hearing me speak. This went on for over two hours before I noticed it was getting late and needed to get home and settled in. He seemed to understand and said he also had another engagement he needed to attend before calling it a night. We both stood and embrace one more time. He planted an innocent on the top of my forehead and I left leaving him standing at the bar.

When I got home I couldn't seem to stop thinking about how natural it was to talk to TJ. I never once felt out of place and like I could just be myself. Yeah, maybe I'll have to keep this in mind when I narrow down who the lucky man will be who I decide to date. I still have one more candidate to see then I would make my decision.

The weekend went by fast and I completed all but one of the two reports I was supposed to. Couldn't stop thinking about the three young men whom I have had the pleasure of seeing thus far. I was once skeptical about this online dating thing but I guess good things can come from it. It I haven't done anything else I've made some good networking connections.

On Monday while sitting in the office checking my e-mails Tyrone, Max and TJ had all left me messages. Each one expressing their interest in me and was wondering if we could possibly go out again. Excitement filled my face causing it to turn beet red. I couldn't believe I had left that everlasting impression on them that they wanted the opportunity to do it again.

I replied back to each one saying, "In due time we will meet again, until then please be patient."

Man, I needed to get this last date out of the way. These men weren't going to keep sticking around if they feel I'm playing games with them. After answering the last e-mail I picked up the phone and dialed Justin's number. He answered on the third ring. "Yo, this Jay what can I do for you?" "Um hello, Justin this is Marissa. Did I catch you at a bad time?" Clearing his throat, "Oh, no I'm sorry I just didn't recognize your number. I thought you may have been a bill collector." We both started laughing. I've done that a million times before too. Pretend to be someone or something else so they would hang up. "I was wondering if you were still interested in going out to have a drink or bit to eat." "That would be great, when are you talking about going?" "How about we meet tomorrow? Say around 6 p.m. I'll meet you there." "That sounds great." He replied.

Justin and I arrived at the same time at the hotel. He opened the door for me and I walked in.   He asked if there was a particular spot I wanted to sit at. Not having one in mind he chose a table in the middle of the bar, in direct view of the stage.   This man must be up to something. Normally I know all the events happening at this spot, but for some reason I must have missed something. Justin pulled out my chair and gestured for me to have a seat. Following his direction I sat in the chair facing the stage. He sat next to me in the chair with a view of the stage also.   The waiter came over to the table and took our order. Justin decided to have a Vodka and Cranberry. Seemed like a good choice and a tad bit risky for me so I ordered one too.   While waiting on our drinks to arrive the MC came on stage and announced tonight was a special night they had a guess performer there to perform. My blood began to race anticipating who this artist could be. Before I could answer my own question the band starting playing music and I knew the tune. Oh no, it couldn't be Uncle Charlie Wilson! Feeling full of excitement I looked at Justin and asked him how he knew Charlie would be there on this night.   He gave me the biggest grin he could possibly give and said, "If I told you then I would have to kiss you." This man was full of surprises. When the drinks arrived at the table the waiter handed me a bouquet of six long stemmed pink, red, and white roses. Each rose had a note attached to it with a different saying on it. Hope-I hope this date is everything you ever wanted and hoped for. Love- True love is what I'm out to find, hope that's what you're searching for too. Peace-Peace of mind, companionship is what I see in you. Faith-It has to be faith that brought us together. Laugh-The way you laugh brighten up my inner being. Beauty-You are a ray of what it means to be beautiful and I see something special in you. My heart melted and tears streamed down my face. Justin handed me a napkin from off the table then rose from his seat, took my hand and lead me to the dance floor. He held me and caressed me in such an erotic way without being disgraceful about it. It was a complete turn on. This was definitely going to be a hard decision. For now I'll just enjoy the moment.

By time I left the bar I was a bit tipsy. Justin offered to call me a cab to ensure I made it home safely. A cab wasn't what I wanted at this moment. A warm gentle body next to mine was what I was wanting. My body was yearning for a male's warm, masculine rock solid body. I hadn't been intimate for well over a year now and it was time. Maybe my co-workers were right I needed a man in my life more than I thought. Tonight would be a great starter to end the drought. What am I thinking? I can't ask them man to my home on the first date. What would he think of me? Right now I don't give a damn what he thinks. He's fine, and available so why not take a shot and ask him over.

"Justin, how about you take me home and stay for a while?" "We could sit and have a cup of coffee or something and just enjoy the remainder of the night together." While slurring each word as I spoke. Justin politely put his arm around my back and drew me close and said, "That would be a great idea but you're in no condition to be entertained and I'm more of a gentleman to not take advantage of a woman who's inebriated and able to make a valid and conscious decision." Stunned and heartbroken I couldn't do anything but respect him for what he said, and it help to sober me up and reality sunk in. I was making a complete fool of myself and willing to give myself up after just a few drinks. I felt ashamed. How could I face this man again after this behavior? "Okay Justin please call me a cab. I'll wait on the inside until I see it pull up." Justin responded, "I'm not going to leave you here by yourself. I'm going to wait right here with you until I see you safely inside the cab." Dropping my head to hide my tears I knew what I needed to do. The cab arrived about 10 minutes after Justine called them and I got in and headed home. Once there I took a hot shower and jumped in the bed. Pulling the covers up over my head to hide my face and drown the memories of that night. It wasn't like me to act out of character like that. Not sure what came over me if it was the liquor or the company of a good looking man who went all out for little ole me.   Staring at the ceiling I slowly drifted off to sleep.

The next morning I sent each of my prospects an e-mail.   I let three of them know that I enjoyed their company and thanked them for taking the time out of their busy schedules to get to know me, but all we could possibly be were friends at this point. My final e-mail was to no other but Justin. I had to apologize for my behavior and beg for his forgiveness. Explaining it was totally out of character for me to act in such a manner was far from normal. Pleading my case I could only hope and pray he understood and would be willing to see me again. All I can do was wait for a response.

I went about my day as normal and I felt a vibration from my phone. It was an email coming through. My hands were full from the groceries I had just purchased I had to wait until I could put them on the corner in the kitchen.   Once my hands were free I quickly pulled my phone from the clip and check the messages. They were from Justin. He told me he understood and could tell I had just gotten caught up in the moment of everything and was just trying to have a good time. Justin said he knew it was something about me and that he wanted to get to know me on even a more personal note. He would be more than please to see me again. Before I could set the phone down my doorbell was ringing. "Who could that be? I'm not expecting any company." Rushing to the door I looked out the peep hole to see who might be standing on the other side. My eyes must be playing tricks on me because the only thing I can see is hundreds of flowers blocking my view. They were roses to be exact. Another knock came at the door. I opened the door and to my surprise Justine walked in and threw the flowers on a table by the door. He then stepped in as close as any person could get invading my personal space and lip locked me with the most passionate kiss I have ever gotten. "I couldn't wait for you to respond or tell me when I could see you again. I need to see you now." Justin said. This man has truly won my heart. I can't believe it. As the wheels were turning in my head Justin had an ulterior motive already in place. He took my hand and said, "Where's the kitchen?" Looking with puppy dog eyes I said, "Over there." We walked into the kitchen and he noticed the groceries I had just purchased. "Go freshen up while I cook you a delicious meal. After dinner I'm going to be your dessert." Wow, I can't believe my ears.

Without any hesitation I rushed into the bedroom and turned on the shower. I then went into my closet to find something nice to put on. By time I had found something suitable to put on I noticed the steam coming from the bathroom meaning my shower had risen to the right temperature. I began to get undressed. Without paying attention I entered the shower and when I pulled back the shower curtain behold a tall, strong succulent body was on the other side. "I wondered what was taking you so long. Get in. I've been waiting on you." Justin said with a malicious grin on his face. "You don't have to tell me twice Justin." Sheepishly I replied. I took the time to admire every inch of Justin's body. From his head, down through the thickness of his neck I touched every inch of him. I wrapped my arms around his waist then stood back to take in the view of his package. I was very impressed by what I saw. Justin had an average size dick but the width of it made up for anything he could be lacking. He began kissing me all over and we made love in the shower until the water ran cold. When finished Justin dried me off with extra care then helped me into the relaxing clothes I had picked out. Justin then told me to go sit in the living room while he prepared dinner. So I did just that.

Justin had the kitchen smelling so delicious. I couldn't wait to see what he had prepared for me. While I waited on the food to get done, Justin handed me a glass of Merlot to drink. He then replied, "This is only the beginning Marissa. If you let me be the man in your life I promise I won't let you down. You'll have no regrets." I could see and feel the sincerity in Justin's eyes, voice and heart. I would be stupid not to give him a chance.

Just when I thought love was lost and internet dating was a roost. Now having experienced it myself I have a totally different outlook on it. There are always the cases where the people you meet online aren't who they say they really are, but it seems I found four really nice men who only wanted to find the right woman to be in their lives. If I had to do it all again; I would do it twice, and to think I almost passed up on the idea. I wouldn't have found my cyber love.

My Biggest Fear

(Love)

I loved you from the beginning

The beginning of our time.

Time together 1999.

That was a time

That sent chills up my spine.

Remembering images of your face,

Of your beauty divine.

My love is strong,

My heart weak,

Sometimes it flutters

Even skips a beat.

It makes a love song,

A ballad so sweet.

Song of a blue humming bird

"do, do, do."

Drawing me out

Of a cocoon-style nest.

Even closer, my dear,

Towards your warm

barren chest.

To feel your embrace

Of your sweet finesse.

I knew from the beginning

One day you'd be mine.

Patience, you said,

It would all fall in line.

I'd overcome my fear

My dear, love from 1999.

To feel your embrace

Or simple caress.

Those are the things

I hold of high interest.

My Secret Love Affair

"Dammit, Jamie!" I shouted. Why can't I seem to get this man out of my head? Jamie was this fine looking brotha who lived down the block from her. He was the most attractive being she had ever laid eyes on. This man stood six foot eight inches tall and had all the masculinity in the world. He has dark short hair, dark mocha skin, smooth, juicy, kissable lips and perfectly straight white teeth. When Jamie would take his shirt off to work on his car all you could see were the outlines of rips and dips of pure muscle. He was as lean as the best cut of meat at the butcher shop. All I knew was he needed to be mine.

I'm Jasmine Mayweather. I live on 108th Avenue and Lennox Blvd in a quiet brownstone apartment. Just recently, I graduated from NYC with a degree in Communications. Currently I'm working part-time at Radio Shack, while looking for a full time gig with a radio station or broadcasting company. I'm 23 years old, no children and no significant other as of yet. Since I've moved to this neighborhood I've had the pleasure of meeting this handsome guy named Jamie Brownlee. One day I was walking from the corner store listening to music through my head phones when I damn near ran him over. I wasn't paying attention and the music had me feeling some type of way. I was grooving and moving in all sorts of ways and didn't pay much attention to the person standing on the sidewalk.

Before I knew it, I was falling all over this man. "Excuse me, I didn't mean to run you over like that." I'm Jasmine Mayweather and I live down the block in those two-toned brownstones. "Oh, you're all right, I saw you were pre-occupied and didn't notice me." Jamie said with a smirk on his face. I'm Jamie Brownlee, and as you can see this is where I reside. Hypnotize! I couldn't say anything else because his beauty had me mesmerized to the point I couldn't talk. I was beyond stunned. This man had it going on!

It seemed like every day after that little incident I looked for Jamie whenever I went out.   Always hoping I would have the opportunity to bump into him once again. His scent was forever entrapped in my skin. The aroma of Usher cologne was to die for. His hormones and the scent of the cologne were a great combination. It made me feel tingly inside and out. I had a "Jones" for this guy. When I went to sleep at night I would dream about this man and couldn't get his face out of my head. The way he touched me the day I damn near plowed over him sent electricity throughout my body causing it to tingle all over. From the sight of this man he had my pussy doing a dance and pulsating at a rate it had never done before. Thinking of the things I would do to him was making me hot and heated. I'm no virgin…that man could truly get the business any day of the week.

I must be crazy to even think that man noticed me. He was only being polite because of how we met, but to have truly noticed me like I did him was a far cry from reality. Nah, he didn't notice me. I'm not the eye grabbing kind of girl. When I look in the mirror all I see is a girl with perfectly flawless medium brown skin, two dimples in each cheek, deep light brown eyes that are deeply set, and short bob-styled hair. I consider myself an "average" looking individual. I'm not a show –stopper like I'm sure he's used to.

To test my hypothesis I began making trips to the corner store a little more frequent than I normally would. There would be times I didn't even need anything from there but would make it seem like I had to go just so I could see Jamie. His scent filled the still air and seemed to make its way into every inch of my nose. When I would get a whiff it made it seem as if I was floating on air. On my way back from one of my many trips to the corner store I felt a pair of eyes homing in on me. As usual I had my headphones on and the music was bumping. On this particular day I was wearing a tight fitting pair of Levi jeans, a half shirt with my school logo on it, and my Space Jam colored Jordan's to match. This time as I was walking, I made sure I kept my ears open and began to look around. Just when I was about to make my way past Jamie's brownstone apartment I spotted someone sitting on the stoup. It was him. He was looking ever so handsome. He had a fresh haircut, had grown his goat-tee out just a little and was wearing some True Religion jeans and matching shirt. As I walked by it appeared his eyes were following me. He wore this devilish grin on his face and was showing those beautiful white teeth. I had to find the nerves to get at this guy. I spoke and he returned the favor. No other words were spoken, but if only he knew how I was feeling about him at that moment, there wouldn't be any need for words only action.

Several days later I was coming out of my apartment to catch the bus for work I noticed Jamie was at the bottom of the steps.

"Hi, what brings you to my humble abode?" I asked.

Jamie looking all around as if he didn't realize I was talking to him. "Oh, I was just in the neighborhood and decided to stop by and see if you wanted to go grab a bite to eat." Jamie replied. I began to giggle.

"In the neighborhood? Really Jamie? Are you for real? You only live down the block you're always in the neighborhood." I responded back in my cutest school girl voice.

Jamie responded back, "Girl, you know I was being sarcastic, but on the real, I do want to have a bite to eat with you."

"I like your style and would love to spend a little time with you to get to know you better."

I damn near pasted out. Those few words took my breath away. "Oh my fucking God this man just asked me out and I've been beating my head in trying to find a way to get this man to notice me." The Lord sure does know how to answer prayers.

I looked at my watch and noticed I only had approximately five minutes before the bus would run and I had about a fifteen minute walk. "Fuck, fuck, fuck!" "What's wrong?" Jamie asked?

"I just realized what time it was, I'm going to be late for work and the bus I normally catch will be here in about five minutes and I have a fifteen minute walk to catch it before it pulls off." Jamie showing those pearly whites said,

"Well how about I give you a lift? That way we can stop and grab a bite to eat?"

"That would be awesome, let me finish locking up and we can go."

We walked down the block to where Jamie lived. His car was parked on the curbside as usual. He drove a hunter green 1978 Camaro. He had stock rims on it and a bra on the front. This car was a classic. He unlocked the car door and then opened it up for me and I proceeded to get in. He then walked around to the driver's side and got in. We pulled off and headed to this quiet little barbeque joint three blocks away. Monroe's BBQ joint was the best place to get your grub on this side of town. The coleslaw was to die for and the way the pulled pork melted in your mouth gave food an entirely new meaning. While I was in college all my classmates talked about was Monroe's. I grew up in Newark and had never tasted anything like this before; so all my friends got together and brought me some back to the dorm. I was in pure heaven by time I finished eating. Ever since then, this has been my secret place to run off to when I'm not feeling my best.

Since I no longer had to catch the bus we decided we had enough time for us to sit down and eat rather than do a take-out order. We laughed and talked for what seemed to be hours. I learned more about Jamie than I ever expected to know. He told me he was 29 years old, had a younger sister named Nina who was a nail tech, he works as a mechanic at a local dealership, has a little 2 year old son named Javier, and had been to prison for 18 months on a simple battery charge. Jamie also told me he has never been married, and his birthday is August 10. He bragged about how good Leo's are and how I should make it my business to get to know one. The entire time he talked he showed off those pretty teeth. I asked him what made him go to prison because I don't view him as the violent type. Jamie responded, "This bitch ass boy decided to put his hands on my sister Nina. That was a wrong move for him so I had to beat his ass to show him who he was fucking with. I will kill for those I love and hold dear to me." I couldn't do anything but respect him for his honesty. If it was me I would do the same exact thing.

It was now my turn to tell Jamie about me. I told him I was 23 years old and had just graduated from NYC with my Bachelors of Science in Communication. I am an only child and my parents live in Newark where I grew up. I currently work at Radio Shack downtown and was looking for a gig with a local radio or broadcasting station. I am currently single, a home body and my birthday is February 14. I am the type of person who believes in love but I don't go out looking for it I feel if it's real then it would find me. Before I could say another word Jamie asked me if I found him attractive. In my mind, I'm saying: "What does he mean do I? Hell yeah I do!" Next thing I know, he leaned in and gave me the wettest kiss I have ever had in my life. It was breathe taking and intense, full of passion. When he finally released my lips from his front teeth I had to shake my head and regain my composure. He then spoke, "So what happened to your last boyfriend may I ask?" Blah, blah, blah was the only thing I could muster up and say. He started to laugh. "That's okay; grab your stuff so I can get you to work. We have plenty of time for you to answer my questions."

On the drive downtown I finally found words to answer the questions Jamie asked of me. I was glowing inside and out and knew I had found a lover in him. As we pulled up to my job he reached over and grabbed my chin and planted yet another kiss on my lips. He then handed me a sheet of paper with his cell phone number written on it. "Don't worry about catching the bus home tonight, call me and I'll be to pick you up." Said Jamie. I wrote down my number on a napkin I had in my pocket and handed it to him. Then I got out the car and nodded my head in agreement to what he had just said. I was giggly on the inside and had a smile as big as the sun on my face. His actions answered all the questions I had been asking myself since I first bumped into him weeks ago. He not only found "me" attractive, but he wanted to spend time with "me" a no-body and it made my heart gleam with joy.

I called Jamie on both of my breaks and we talked and laughed like we had known each other for years. I informed him that I was in charge of closing the store tonight and had to do inventory afterwards and told him I hoped it wasn't too late for him to pick me up. As I had already told my other two co-workers they could go home early and I would take care of the store. Normally one of them would stay and walk with me to the bus stop to make sure I was safe. They repeatedly asked if I was sure and I confirmed to them "yes." I'm sure; I have someone coming to pick me up. I knew this would draw their suspicions of who this mystery person could possibly be. I love the two I work with on a regular but they are some nosey people.

Towards the close of business the store got real busy for some strange reason. I sold more items within the last 20 minutes of the store being open than I had all day. Maybe this was a sign things were looking up for me. I could only hope at this point. Ten thirty rolled around and Jamie was pulling up in front of the store. He watched me as I locked up the store and he got out of the car, walked around to the passenger side and opened up the door for me. Once I was in comfortably he closed the door then walked back around to the driver's side and we pulled off.

"How was your night?" asked Jamie.

"It was good. I got a little busy towards the end of my shift, but overall it was a decent night." Jamie then asked if I was hungry and wanted to stop and get a bite to eat. I told him I was okay and just wanted to get home and take a hot shower then curl up under my blanket then watch a movie. Jamie mumbled under his breathe, "Wish I could take a hot shower with you." That put a bigger smile on my face. I pretended I didn't hear him and stared straight ahead the remainder of the drive to my place. When he pulled up he parked the car and turned the ignition off. He then turned his body so he could look directly at me and said, "I know you heard what I said and I'm waiting on an answer. Can I come up and join you in that hot shower you're about to take?" This man is unbelievable. My instincts are saying no it's too soon to have this man in your place, but my body was saying, you better tell him yeah before he finds someone else to take a shower with. I quickly nodded my head yes and got out the car.

Jamie followed me as quickly as he could. I opened the door to my apartment and left the door wide open for him. He came in stripping all of his clothes off showing that chiseled body I love so much. I was trying to get to the bathroom to turn on the shower, but Jamie stopped me by grabbing my arm and spinning me around, planting a deep, long, passionate kiss on my lips. His tongue was so far down my throat I had trouble swallowing. I felt my knees giving from up under my body and he quickly caught me and picked me up and carried me into the bathroom shutting the door behind us. He turned me around placing my back against the door and began undressing me with his teeth. My pussy was quickly heating up I couldn't resist this man's touch. In no time Jamie had me standing butt ass naked in the bathroom and he stood back to admire my body. "Um hmm, delightful and succulent." He exhaled. He planted his juicy wet lips on the tip of my nipples making his way around my entire areola.

The passion he used when he sucked my breast had my body feeling tingly and weak. I needed for him to stop so I could compose myself but I also needed this man at this very moment. While he was sucking on my breast with one hand he undid the button on his jeans and had them wrapped around his ankles in record time. He released my breasts from his lips and stood back. I couldn't help but to admire the girth of this man's penis. It was so large and thick. I couldn't believe he was packing a fucking 10 inch long 6 inch wide dick in them jeans. Who would have ever thought he had all that going on. Don't know how I'm going to take all of that but I guarantee you once I get it I'm going to keep on getting this dick. My head was spinning a hundred miles an hour, but I knew I was about to partake in an adventurous ride of a lifetime.

I could feel the steam from the shower causing the temperature in the bathroom to rise. The mirrors began to cloud up and so was my body core. I'm more than positive if someone was to take my temperature at this very moment it would read well over 105 degrees. My pussy was swelling up and juices were beginning to flow. Jamie must have been reading my mind. He guided me into the shower and washed, caressed, touch, pinched and kissed every inch of my body. It was tantalizing and hypnotic. I was falling so hard for this guy. I know I need to reevaluate this situation and not rush anything but I was hooked from the first time I laid eyes on him. Here he is in my bathroom taking me on a fantastic ride like no other man has ever done. It felt wonderful.

We made love in the shower, on the floor, standing and when it finally had gotten too heated in the bathroom we made our way to my king sized bed and used up every inch of it. This man had given me more orgasms than I have ever experienced in my entire time having sex. He knew exactly what he was doing and how I was responding moaning and groaning, arching my back and sweating like a Hebrew slave. There was nothing I could do or say at this moment. I was spent.

After hours of love making, we fell asleep holding each other. The last thing I remember was Jamie kissing me on my forehead telling me how he had a great time and wanted to see me on a more regular basis. I told him that would be great and drifted off to sleep. When I woke the next morning Jamie was gone. He left his shirt with a note attached to it.

"Sorry I had to leave so soon, work calls. I'll be by later to finish what we started last night. Here are a few dollars for you to get a bite to eat and catch the bus to work." - Jamie.

I unfolded the bills and counted them, $100.00. Wow! No one had ever left me that kind of money before. Boy do I feel special. I looked at the time on the clock it read 6:45

a.m. I decided to roll back over and get a few more minutes of sleep. When I woke back up, it the clock read 8:15 a.m. I'd better rush now I have to be at work in 2 hours and need to grab a bite to eat. I forced myself to make my way into the bathroom, turned on the shower. The aroma of sex still filled the air in the shower area. We most definitely did some things while in here. Giggling. While the shower was heating up I decided to explore my closet to find something to wear to work. I decided on a red see through blouse and black slacks. Found my name tag in my purse and adhered all items I found necessary for the day.

Several minutes later I headed back into the bathroom and took a long overdue shower. Flashbacks from the night before filled my head and placed a smile on my face. Who would have thought he would notice someone like "me."

Oh well, can't worry about that, the point is he did and just didn't care. I could feel myself smiling the entire walk to the bus hub and then again the entire time I rode the bus. It's going to be very obvious when I walk into work what happened to me, but I really didn't care at this point. I couldn't hide the smile that was entrancing my face. I had gotten the man I dreamed of and wanted for some time now. I don't care if the entire world finds out. I've been alone for way too long and it my time to have someone in it if only for a short time. Jamie was the oldest man I have ever dated and for him to take interest in me was an accomplishment.

When I arrived at work I was wearing the same Kool aid grin I had been all morning. My two favorite co-workers had already opened the store and were assisting a few customers. Walking in I said, "Hello" to everyone and proceeded to the back to put my items in the back storage room. As I was walking I overheard Jessie telling Craig about this abusive ex-boyfriend. I kept walking as if I didn't hear what they were talking about. As I was hanging up my jacket, the first person to come in the back was my home girl, Jessie.

"So, Miss Thang what's with this Chester Cheetah grin you wearing?"

"I don't know what you're talking about Jessie. It's a beautiful day outside and I'm enjoying being alive, that's all."

"Oh, come on Jas you ain't fooling anyone it's written all over your face. It must be that new mystery man who's been picking you up."

"Maybe it is maybe it ain't either way it's my business and until I'm ready to speak on it, we'll just leave it where it's at." I replied. Jessie storms out of the back room with tear stained face.

"What's her problem?" I asked Craig. "She's just upset Jas, somehow her abusive ex-boyfriend found out where she lives and works. She scared for her life." Craig Responded. I never knew Jessie had an abusive ex. We've all hung out together after work but she's never mentioned she was abused by her ex-boyfriend. I feel so bad for her. I'm going to give her the rest of the day off and let her compose herself. I'll go by her house on my lunch break and check on her. She has me worried.

Every few minutes I would look at the clock to check the time. Jessie was on my mind and I couldn't shake it. When it was time for my lunch break I walked the four blocks to where Jessie stayed. I banged on the door and she wouldn't answer. I became even more worried…what if this man had come and done something horrible to her? Maybe I should have inquired what it was she and Craig were talking about when I first walked in, but I was too caught up trying to enjoy my own moment that I didn't ask.

I walked back to Radio Shack and told Craig about Jessie not being home when I arrived. He didn't look surprised at all. Wondering what could have happened I questioned Craig. "Did you know she wouldn't answer the door and you knew I was going over to check on her?" Silence filled the room. Craig had his head bowed down and he slowly raised it up. "Jas, you just don't understand what all Jessie has been through."

"You're right I don't, but I want to understand." I shouted in a brusque tone. Once again Craig looked me in the eyes and said, "Jessie saw you with your new lover/boyfriend the other night when he came to pick you up."

I do not understand what he means. "What difference does it make if Jessie saw me with my date?"

Craig with the look of disbelief on his face cried out, "Because it's her abusive ex you were with!!!"

Storming out of the store with tears streaming down my face, I couldn't believe what my ears just heard. How could this be? Jamie doesn't seem like the type of person to harm a fly. I had to get to the bottom of this. I pulled my cell phone out and called Jamie and told him to meet me at the corner of Saks 5th and Montgomery. Standing by the corner pacing I spotted the green Camaro from a block away. Jamie pulled up and opened the door from the inside and I got in. He then leaned in as if to give me a kiss and I quickly pulled away.

"What's wrong beautiful, I was worried when you called?" Asked Jamie.

"Just drive, Jamie we will talk once we get to my place!"

We drove in silence and I contemplated the questions in my head that I wanted to ask him. Minutes later we pulled up at my brownstone. I got out of the car and slammed the door and ran up the stairs to my place. Jamie ran full speed up the stairs after me. When he entered the apartment I was balled up on the couch in a fetal position crying my eyes out. Not knowing what to do Jamie held me and asked why I was so upset. My nose running and sniffling I found the voice to tell him the information I was given. Jamie was appalled.

He looked me in the eyes and kissed my face and said, "Baby, it's not me. I swear to you I have never in my life seen or known this woman. She has to be mistaken." Jamie came even closer to me and began undressing me. He kissed me from the top of my head to the soles of my feet. He made love to me in a way I was yet prepared for. It was mind blowing and invigorating. Unfortunately, that wasn't enough; I was still confused and didn't know what to believe. After we finished an intense love session, I turned to Jamie and told him I need for him to come to my job so Jessie could make a positive identification and prove him wrong. I couldn't continue seeing this man if he is a liar and abusive to his women.

Jamie agreed and several days later he met me at my job. I had him come around 3p.m. since I knew Jessie would be getting off at 4. He walked into the store and Jessie was the first person to spot him. She froze up and began yelling. "Get the fuck outta here! How dare you come to my place of employment to try to intimidate me? You fucking bastard."

I ran from the back to see what was going on and grabbed Jas to calm her. "Jessie what's wrong this here is my friend Jamie and I told him about the mix up and he came to prove to you he doesn't know you."

"So that's what he's calling himself? That bitch name is not no damn Jamie its James and he lives on Maryland Drive and Oyster St." yelled Jessie.

"Now hold the fuck up young lady! I've never laid eyes on you before until this very moment. You have me mixed up with someone else and whoever it is, it ain't me." Jamie egregiously responded. "And, for the record, I've never lived in that neighborhood you claim I do. Just ask your girl where I live, she will vouch for me."

Everyone stood looking stunned. Jas walked over to me and grabbed me at my collar on my shirt. "You have got to believe me. I wouldn't lie about something like this." Torn I didn't have any words to speak or the knowledge to know the truth. What I did know was we had to get to the bottom of this. I couldn't have my friend and co-worker scared to death like this. In mid thought Jessie's phone rung. She looked at the name on the caller ID and then showed me. "It's him, what do I do?" I've got to think fast. "Answer the phone, put it on speaker and act normal."

Jessie answered the phone and the caller began yelling obscenities. Jessie was so nervous she hung the phone up. Next thing we know a man came barging into the store and we all froze. Jamie was looking just as stunned as we were. We were seeing double. How could this be? Twins?

"Bitch don't you ever hang up on me again. If you do I'll kill you!" barked the stranger.

Jamie rushed the guy asking him who the hell he was and why in the hell did he look just like him. As far as Jamie knew he only had a sister, but this fool was a splitting image of him. Jessie ran off leaving us all to deal with this cat. Craig had unknowingly to us called the police and they soon barged in the store a few minutes later. We soon discovered the man's name was James and he was given away at birth. James had been the one who dated Jessie and was the abusive boyfriend she had been talking about and not my Jamie. We were all pleased to find that information out.

The police arrested James and took him down to the station. Come to find out, several other women had filed complaints about him and he was a wanted man. We were all ecstatic to find out the news and to have this criminal off the streets. Jamie was sad and wanted some answers also. Craig called one of the other stores and asked them if they would send someone over to help run the store. He then told me to take the remainder of the day off, go find Jessie and give her the good news and be supportive of my man. I took that advice and did just that. Craig handed me my jacket from the back room and I grabbed Jamie's hand and we left.

Once in the car, I asked Jamie if he was going to be okay. He assured me he would be. I was doubtful so I leaned in and planted a kiss on his cheek and told him I was there for him. He smiled showing those beautiful teeth I love to see, and we pulled off. Jamie drove to the outer part of the city and didn't speak a word. I could tell his mind was racing a thousand mile an hour so I let him have his peace.

Soon we pulled up at this set of duplexes and parked. Jamie got out the car and walked over to my side and opened the door. He held my hand to assist me getting out of the car. Once out, he planted a deep passionate kiss on my lips and told me this was where his mother lived and he needed for her to give him some answers. Shaking my head up and down I knew this visit wasn't to say hi and keep it moving. This particular visit maybe his last if he didn't hear the answers he wanted to hear.

"Don't worry beautiful we won't be here very long. Mama only has a few seconds to tell me what I want to hear then we're out." Jamie said.

Before we could even knock on the door, it swung flying open. There at the door stood a petite woman of 5'1 inches tall with her hair covered with a bonnet. Jamie didn't say a word he just pushed his way pass her. Jamie went in the living room and sat on the couch. He waited for her to come in before he started in on her. By the look on her face she knew what this visit was about.

"I'm sorry baby; I didn't want you to find out about your brother like this." I was only a teenage girl when I got pregnant with you and turning tricks to get by. I gave up your brother so he could have a good home and a family to love him." She cried.

"Cut the bullshit mama. You could have told me long before now I was a twin. You see the shit he's out here doing to women. I could never do something like that. I could have gone back to prison for this type of shit. You got my girl all concerned and not trusting me. What kind of mess is that? How could you do this to me?" Jamie sobbed with crocodile tears in his eyes.

I jumped up from the chair I was sitting in and wrapped my arms around him as tight as I could. "It's okay baby, I'm here for you. When you ready to go just nod your head and we can leave." Jamie then nodded his head and we left.

We drove back to my place. Jamie was distraught by the news he received from his mom. Pondering what I could do to console him I did the only thing I knew to do. I undressed Jamie and kiss his body all over. When I got down to his pants I rubbed my lips over his zipper where his dick sat. I slowly undid the zipper and reached inside his pants and pulled out his thick, succulent dick.

Using both hands I began to massage it. Wetting up my lips I slowly place them on the head of his dick and lowered my mouth all over it. I began to suck and slob on it slowly. He must have been enjoying himself because he passionately grabbed the back of my head to assist with the motion. Faster and faster, deeper and deeper I took that dick in my mouth. When he had enough he pulled me up and placed me on the floor next to where we stood. He spread my legs open and removed my panties. He opened up the lips to my pussy and began to lick sending chills up and down my body. I loved what he was doing to me.

He climbed on top of me and forced his dick into my pussy and it instantly began to flow my precious juices. I was whipped and this man meant the world to me. I can't believe I didn't give him the benefit of the doubt before not trusting him. This love making session would surely make up for all the doubt. We made love until the sun came up the next day.

Early the next morning my phone rang and it was Jessie calling to apologize for the mix-up. I told her anyone could have done the same. She wished me the best with my relationship with Jamie and I thanked her for her support. Not feeling my best I jumped up and ran to the bathroom. Jamie rushed in behind me to see if I was alright. I told him I had missed my period this month. He looked at me with sparkles in his eyes. "I'm going to be a daddy!" he yelled.

Then he got down on one knee and pulled this small black box from behind his back. He then took my hand and looked me dead in the eyes and proceeded to ask, "Miss Jasmine Mayweather would you do me the honor of being my wife?" Tears flowing from my face I answered, "Yes!"

Six months had passed by from the time of this entire ordeal began. I had gotten my man and found out I was having his baby. Jamie no longer went to visit his mom, but he told her about the baby we were expecting. Jessie no longer worked at the store and moved to D.C. with her parents, and life was good. Jamie was waiting on me hand and foot and our love making sessions never seemed to get old. I knew from the first time I laid eyes on this man I was in love. For all this to come true is only a blessing from God.

Wonder Twins

(Power of the Pussy)

"Fuck, I need to call my sis Karmen and tell her to bring her ass over here expeditiously. I got this nigga over here talking shit about he can take the both of us on. He must not know who the hell he dealing with, because the Montague sisters don't play about no dick." Sasha said yelling into the air. Shit let me find my phone and give her a call.

Sasha Montague is the younger, vibrant and intelligent sister of Karmen, but if you didn't know any different you would swear they were identical twins. Karmen is considered the more outgoing and spontaneous of the two. She's not afraid to try new things at least once. These two sisters would complete each other's sentences and often feel the pain the other one would experience. The two were inseparable.

Not only do these sisters share secrets, clothes, or hair products from time to time they share certain men as well. They only had one stipulation when it came to the men they introduced to one another: If either one caught feelings for the man or found themselves in love with him he was off limits for a lifetime. What's understood between the sisters didn't need any explanation. They had a special bond, one no one could break. Each one had productive careers during the day, but turned freaks at night.

Sasha was five foot two inches tall, dark complexion, long black flowing hair, dark brown doe eyes, slim waist, and size 44G breast. While Karmen, the older sister stood at five foot three inches tall, caramel complexion, short bob-styled hair, light brown wide eyes, big round butt and solid firm size 38DDD breast. These sisters had it going on.

"Shit this damn phone is at the bottom of this big ass purse. I knew better than to put it in there." Sasha says while digging in her purse. I sure hope Karmen answers her damn phone. She's good at call screening. This bitch would be right by the phone and lean over to see who it is calling and ignore the ring. Today I need for her to pick up 'cause we got some business to handle. Ain't no man gone call me and my sister out about our sex game and we don't handle up. He better learn to recognize he ain't playing with any rookies. If we decided to sell this shit between our legs we both would be billionaires. Not to mention the fire ass head game. Once my sister showed me a technique on how to swallow the entire dick by arching my mouth and tickling my gag reflexes, shit I've mastered it ever since. She had me practicing on pickles, bananas and dildos.

I can remember the first time I asked Karmen how to suck the dick she looked at me and said, "Sash you need to stop playing. I know well and good you know how to suck some dick. As much as you fuck you can't tell me you just now experimenting with sucking dick." Looking like a lost child I looked up at her and replied, "Nah sis, I can fuck a mean dick but I've never experienced sucking one. The men I deal with don't really ask for any head they just want the pussy so it's never been a big deal that I don't suck dick." Karmen begins to laugh softly, and then says, "How long did you think you were going to keep fucking these men before they tell you to start sucking their dick?" "All men love to get their dicks sucks and their balls massaged. You need to stop acting so prissy and get with the program. Haven't you heard, what you won't do they will find a hoe that will?" I guess Karmen had a valid point. I needed to step my game up, my head game that is.

Oh, finally Karmen's phones ringing. She breaks my thoughts when she answered on the second ring. "What Sasha? Don't you know it's my day off? Why the fuck you calling me at this hour" rudely asked Karmen. "Look Karmen, I got this nigga over here talking about we ain't shit and that he could take the both of us on." "You know I don't play about this sex shit so let's show this fool how the Wonder Twins get down." I responded with a sigh. "All right

Sasha. I'll be over in a few, let me get dressed first."

Within the next half hour or so Karmen was knocking at the door. "Come in, Karmen I'm in the den." I yelled while out of view. Karmen made her way to the back of my house where she found me in a spare bedroom searching for something seductive to put on. "What the fuck are you doing Sasha? You had me come all the way over here and yo ass ain't even dress. You have got to be kidding me." Karmen said boisterously. "Just give me a second sis I needed to make sure I left an everlasting impression on this fool, I promise I'll be ready shortly." I responded.

"If I didn't love my sister as much as I do. I'd leave her ass and make her handle this nigga by herself. I was resting comfortably before she called with this nonsense, but I'm all in for a good fucking so what the heck."- Karmen.

"I'm about ready to go sis. How do I look?" I asked with a malice grin on my face. "You look like a hoe, but I love it, you've got me feeling overly dressed." Chuckled, Karmen. My sister had found this sexy black laced, see through body suit. She had matching 5 inch stilettos to match with feathers flying all over. I must say I wasn't ready for her. I felt overly dressed in my cream colored tight fitting leather outfit with matching 5 inch stilettos. Checking myself over to make sure I didn't need a wardrobe change, Sasha finished applying her makeup and quickly grabbed her keys. Since she knew where we were going we decided to take her car, plus it was better on gas mileage then the SUV I drove.

We laughed and joked about the last fool we tag teamed. It wasn't anything nice. He also thought he would call us out about our sexual capabilities and how we weren't shit. Just bragging how he would have us both screaming and calling him daddy. Fuck that! I quickly let the fool know I have one daddy and he's the only one to receive that name. Sorry buddy you ain't him.

The things Sasha and I did to that man we would truly take to our graves. While I was pussy fucking his face, Sasha was sucking his dick until he thought she had removed his entire foreskin. After this went on for about fifteen minutes or so we switched. My head game was twice as better than Sasha so I had this fool squirming like a little bitch. My mouth opened wide to show my double tongue piercing, I commenced to tickle the head of his dick, making circular motions. Gently moving down his shaft; a little at a time until I was able to consume his entire dick in my mouth. I would deep throat his dick then go slow then fast speeding up with each motion. Using my hands I would massage his balls as I'm sucking. When I grabbed his ass and began to run my index finger between his butt hole and scrotum adding friction with each movement this man began to convulse and flop around like a gold fish.

Once I had this fish right where I wanted him I got up and straddled his dick backwards in a cowboy position. Sasha was tongue kissing him in the mouth and sucking on his chest. He was finger fucking Sasha's pussy causing her juices to flow everywhere. In mid stride Sasha and I slapped hands and did our little saying, "Wonder Twin powers, activate." This man didn't know what to think of what was happening to him. Sasha and I simultaneously switched positions and now she was riding his dick. Sasha was throwing her pussy at him like she was riding a raging bull. Bucking and jerking with each movement. Dude was spent. We could tell he was about to explode by the expressions on his face and the way he was jerking about, so Sasha jumped up and started jacking him off. In a matter of a few seconds this fool was nutting all over the place. Sasha and I calmly walked and grabbed our clothes and left him where he laid.

When we set out to handle our business we don't half step about anything. Having male mentality and coming from an overly sexual father who taught his daughters by any means necessary we aim to please. We have to live up to the Montague name. Pops Buck Montague was said to be a beast in the bedroom from what we heard. So it must be a natural trait that we inherited his genes and a high sex drive. Many of the women he's been with say the stamina of that man is like a race horse. He never gets tired and when he bust that first nut he ready to go again. All Sasha and I could do was laugh. Yeah we got it honestly.

My thoughts were broken when the car abruptly stopped at this house over on the Northside of town. "We're here." Sasha said. It wasn't the best neighborhood in the world but it wasn't the worst either. This bum ass dude lives in a rundown house where the shutters are falling off and the paint is chipped around the trimming. He has the audacity to say we ain't shit? By the looks of things he ain't shit and his house proves it. Like I said he doesn't know who or what he about to get himself into. Sasha lives in this cute 2 bedroom 2 ½ bath condo on the out skirts of town and I own this nice little 3 bedroom 3 bath 2 car garage bungalow ten miles outside the city limits. We we're anything to be bargained with.

"Let's go sis. It's time to handle this dude, and then go for some drinks." Said Sasha.

"You're right, let's get this over with so we can have a real three some." I said jokingly. Our three some would consist of Jose Cuervo, 1800 silver and Patron tequila. These men always made us feel some type of way whenever we got together.

We both got out of the car and closed the doors behind us. Walking up to the house Sasha knocked on the door. A dark skinned, average built man wrapped in a blue bath towel answered the door. A ball of smoke rolled out of the house and the smell of weed encompassed my nose. My eyes instantly bucked when I noticed the bulge in the middle of the towel. Hmm he must have had to get one off before the show began. It would be the only way he would be able to handle the two of us. I'm very positive he's going to be very disappointed in his performance. To make sure he does; I made sure I brought my little bag of tricks.

Sasha introduced us as we walked in the house. Terry say hello to my sister Karmen, the one I've been telling you about. Doesn't she look as hot as I described her to be? Terry giving me the once over licks his lips and replies, "Hell yeah she looks hot and even better now that I've seen her in person." Terry begins rubbing his dick as if neither one of us is standing there. "What are y'all ladies waiting on? Let's get this party started; y'all didn't come over here for us to be staring at each other." Said Terry. Sasha was the first to speak up. "Hell nah nigga we ain't come all the way over here to be looking at each other. Shit if I wanted something to look at I could have stayed at home in the bed watching my 70 inch flat screen TV." "I second that motion." Cosigning on what Sasha said. "Where's a damn drink? I need to get my throat wet before we begin this sexcapade." "Look in the kitchen on the counter. I'm sure you'll find something you like." Yelled Terry.

While I was in the kitchen pouring me a drink, Sasha decided she was going to get the party started early. Terry and her went into the back bedroom and began an all-out fuck feast. You could hear the slapping and pounding of his dick against her ass. Terry was yelling obscenities "Fuck me bitch, make this pussy make some noise." I believe I heard Sasha laugh a time or too. She was making a fool of this man. After a few more minutes the both of them came out of the room.

Sasha looked at me and said, "Your turn. Show him what you working with sis."

That was my cue. I was full off of that drink I had made for myself and was ready for some dick. Terry insisted that I got on top. He didn't know that was one of my favorite positions. I rode his dick until he thought he had lost all feeling. I bucked and jerked and pounded my pussy against his lower abdomen. My pussy was good and wet. He rolled over and said, "Get on your back, fuck this I'm about to eat this pussy like it's my last meal." Terry obviously high attempted to rub my clit with his fingers but kept missing the spot. I started to get agitated with his attempts. I then took his head and forced his mouth down on my pussy and demanded that he suck, lick then suck some more. This nigga's face was covered with my juices but I wasn't finished with him yet. I yelled for Sasha to come in the room and bring my gift bag.

Sasha entering the room butt ass naked with only the duffle bag in tow. "Unzip the bag and hand me my tool." Sasha knew exactly which tool I was speaking of. With Terry still face down in my pussy I turned on the anal vibrator and handed it back to Sasha. Put the scrotum cuffs on his balls first then proceed with care. Terry tried to jump up but I had my legs wrapped around his neck so tight he couldn't go anywhere.

Once the cuffs were secure around Terry's balls I placed gel onto the vibrator that Sasha was holding. She then gently opened up Terry's ass cheeks and began sliding the vibrator up and down his ass. He didn't flinch. Seeing how he was actually beginning to enjoy the show I nodded to my sister, put it in his ass. Right on command Sasha shoved the vibrator up Terry's ass and he clinched onto my clit so hard I had an instant orgasm. It was a painful type of pleasure but well worth it. We then turn him onto his back and began fucking him like we were on a sea saw. I rode his face and she rode his dick while holding hands and playing patty cake. This continued for about five more minutes before a muffled tone came from up under me. "I'm about to bust. Fuck, shit, dammit here it comes." Sasha and I laughed so hard our stomachs ached. Our mission was complete. Bet he won't talk about we ain't shit to no one else. We grabbed our clothes and left just as easily as we came.

We both went home to soak in a hot bubble bath and I poured me up another drink. As I laid back in my full size garden tub I thought about the games and tricks Sasha and I would pull on these lame ass men who claim their dicks are made of steel, but only to be broken down into infant status once my sister and I tag teamed they ass. No longer would they be able to brag about how good their sex was or how they're the baddest pussy eater this side of town. When they see us in public driving down the street they won't even look our way.

All of this was getting old to me. I was getting tired of using my pussy as a weapon. No matter how much sex I got in a weeks' time, nothing would compare to getting it from someone to call your own.

The next morning while I was preparing myself for work, my Snapchat was buzzing and Sasha's picture displayed on the screen. She knows I hate getting calls first thing in the mornings. I should ignore her ass, but it wouldn't do any good she would only keep calling until I answered. "What is it Sasha? What can I do for you on this fine morning?" I snapped. "Gosh sis. What's with you; and a good morning to you too?

Did you sleep well last night?" Sasha inquired in her high pitched voice. "Blah, I guess you can say that. Sasha how many times have I told you I don't like calls first thing in the morning? You know I'm not the best morning person." I barked. "Oh Karmen, technically I didn't call you, this is video chat there's a difference." Sashed snickered maliciously. "You better be glad you're my sister or I'd hang the hell up on your smart ass."

Couldn't help but, laugh at my own remarks. "What's on your mind, Sasha?" Sasha, "I was thinking about how we did ole boy last night. I tried to call him this morning and do you know the nigga had the nerve to change his damn number?" We both busted out in laughter. "Fucking Idiot! That'll teach his ass." -Karmen responded.

The day went on and Karmen's mind continued to be in deep thought. She wanted out of this little side business her and Sasha had going on. How would she break the news to Sasha? She was the one who introduced Sasha to this lifestyle and now she's hooked. She even enjoys what she does to these men. The only complaint is neither one was getting paid for their services; they were basically giving away their skills and getting nothing in return. Yeah they would have complete control over the man involved, but he's the one receiving all the benefits. He's living out a fantasy he probably thought would never happen, and all the women leaves with is a wet ass.

Buzz, buzz, and buzz. My thoughts were broken up by the sound of the vibration of my cell phone. Looking at the caller ID I recognized the number. It was this guy named C.J. I secretly admired. Sasha and I started out several years ago plotting to break C.J. He was one of those conceded brothas who was under the assumption every woman wanted him and he was top shit. There was a time I couldn't wait to break him down and expose him for the pussy he really was. Unfortunately, things took a turn at a different angle.

Sasha and I witnessed C.J. get mugged in a parking garage one day. We saw how he pleaded for help and the innocence of his voice and seeing him lying helpless changed our mind. We scratched him off the list instantly and vowed to never attempt to conquer him ever. Somehow C.J. discovered I was the one who called 911 and ran to get help. He's now here at my job unannounced bearing gifts. He told me he knew it was me and appreciated what I had done. The small bit of humbleness and sincerity in his cry for help changed my perception of him. Ever since that incident, I've had this huge crush on the man.

He walks into my office and before I could tell him to have a seat my cell phone goes off. I held my index finger up to tell C.J. to give me just a second and I would be right with him. "Sasha what is it? I have a client in my office at the moment."

"Karmen this is a 911 call we got another job to do. I need you to come to 2478 N. Division St. on your lunch break and bring your tools." Sasha barked out.

I looked up at C.J. who sat with this puzzled look on his face. I didn't know what to say or how to respond. I was interested in this man sitting in front of me and wouldn't mind settling down but my loyalty is with Sasha and she needs me. How do I get out of this mess and have the man I yearn for at the same time? This was going to be harder than I anticipated.

C.J. and I talked for over the next hour or so. We were enjoying each other's conversation and I was really feeling this guy. I just happened to check my watch and it was a quarter to one. "Shit", I yelled time had slipped away. "I understand you're a busy lady Karmen. I just wanted to show you my gratitude and let you know I've got my eye on you. I wouldn't mind taking you out and have a couple of drinks with to get to know each other better." C.J. replied. "Yes, we must do that C.J. I'll call you and let you know what my schedule is looking like so we can set something up."

Once he left my office I gathered my items and headed out the door. I told my secretary that I would be a little late returning from lunch and to take all my calls. Rushing over to the address Sasha had given me I was thinking of ways I could tell her this would be my last job. I was retiring and ready to settle down. I'm sure she would understand but be heartbroken at the same time. We had been doing this type of thing for quite some time now and she looked up to me. Soon I pulled up at the house and saw that Sasha was already there. I parked my car and turned off the engine. Gave Sasha a coded text letting her know I was there.

Right when I was about to press send she tapped on the passenger side window and nodded her head signaling for us to go in. Unlike the last lame's home this one was actually immaculate. I was impressed. Almost made me hate I was getting out of the business. These type of individuals

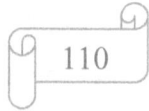

normally begged to give us a little "settlement money" for our troubles.

Sasha knocked on the door and we entered. Once inside, we both noticed there were four glasses of wine on the bar, food spread out on the table next to it and music playing. Maybe this time we in over our heads but time would only tell. I began admiring all the art work on the walls. Whoever lived here had great taste. Then I heard a voice I recognized. "It couldn't be who I'm thinking it is." I yanked Sasha by the arm to get her attention. "Sasha tell me who the fuck lives in this house? You know you're always supposed to notify me about the guys you pick for us." Angrily I gripped. "Oh, Karmen. Chill out it's that guy we were supposed to set straight a few years back what's the big deal?"

I have got to get out of here before he notices me and my chance with him is over. Unfortunately, I was too late getting to the door before I could turn the knob C.J. tapped me on my shoulder and asked why I was leaving the party so soon. I was embarrassed and didn't have any words. I felt bad for what was taking place and now he knows what I do part-time. He would never forgive me, or I myself. Sasha walks over and says, "Come on you two we have a celebration to get started." Why are you still standing by the door? "Karmen, I know you been telling me how much you wanted out so here is your chance for happiness. I wish you nothing but the best and you'll always be my number one Wonder Twin."

I couldn't believe Sasha had set this entire thing up. I'm glad she did. I'm not getting any younger and settling down is what I want and need. Not sure how she knew I was head over heels for this man, but I'm glad she did and could feel how I was feeling. I love this chic to infinity and beyond.

About the Author

Keeta B. is the Author of the recently released book Life's Memories. She brings to you a new twist of writing with *Unforeseen Partitions*. She collaborated with a new and upcoming writer Keybae (Malissa Borders-Hinnant) who wrote an expiring erotic poem and looks forward to bringing more avenues of work to her readers soon.